For Sheniz and Noah ~ C. F.

For Nia ~ B. C.

ALADDIN

An imprint of Simon & Schuster Children's Publishing Division

1230 Avenue of the Americas, New York, NY 10020

This Aladdin hardcover edition May 2016

Text copyright © 2015 by Claire Freedman

Illustrations copyright © 2015 by Ben Cort

Published by arrangement with Simon & Schuster UK Ltd.

Originally published in Great Britain in 2015 by Simon & Schuster UK Ltd.

All rights reserved, including the right of reproduction in whole or in part in any form.

ALADDIN is a trademark of Simon & Schuster, Inc., and related logo is a

registered trademark of Simon & Schuster, Inc.

For information about special discounts for bulk purchases, please contact

Simon & Schuster Special Sales at 1-866-506-1949 or business@simonandschuster.com.

The Simon & Schuster Speakers Bureau can bring authors to your live event.

For more information or to book an event contact the Simon & Schuster Speakers Bureau

at 1-866-248-3049 or visit our website at www.simonspeakers.com.

Designed by Karina Granda

Manufactured in China 1215 LEO

2 4 6 8 10 9 7 5 3 1

Library of Congress Control Number 2015952129

ISBN 978-1-4814-6736-0 (hc)

ISBN 978-1-4814-6737-7 (eBook)

• The Underpants Books •

Aliens Love Dinopants

ILLUSTRATED BY
Ben Cort

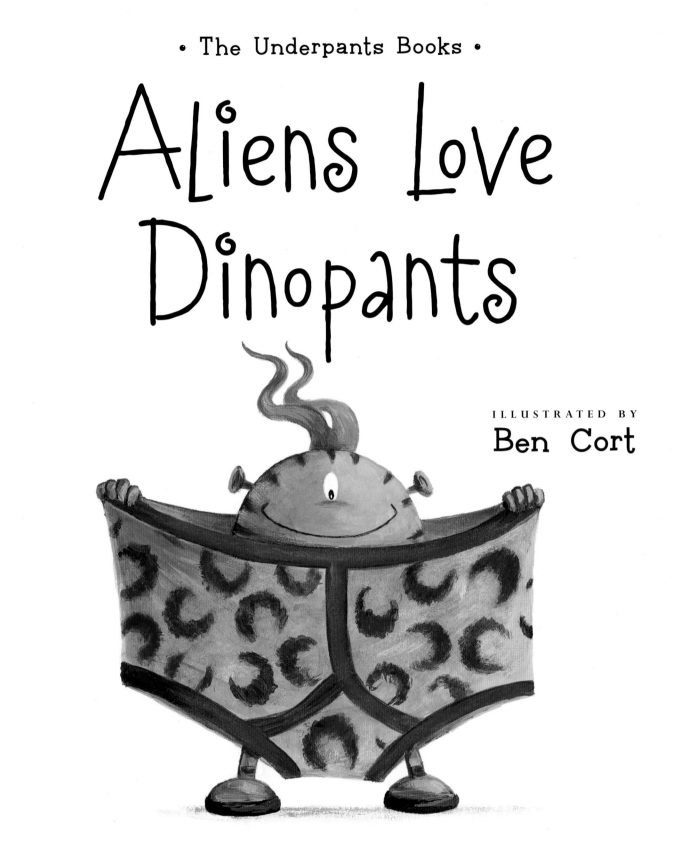

CLAIRE FREEDMAN

aladdin

NEW YORK   LONDON   TORONTO   SYDNEY   NEW DELHI

A band of pants-mad aliens
Zoomed down here, when SURPRISE!
Bright lightning hit their spaceship, *BANG!*
And hurled them from the skies.

Crash-landing in thick jungle,

"Whoops!" the aliens gasped. "Oh dear!"

But their pants-tracker was BLEEPING.

How could underpants be here?

The aliens trekked through tangly trees,
The signal getting stronger.
Through slimy swamps, down deep ravines,
Could they go on much longer?

Their tracker just went BONKERS!

"Wow! We must be close," they cried.

It led them to a hidden gate.

"Let's take a peek inside!"

BLEEP! BLEEP! YIPPEE!

They'd found them!

(Those aliens are so clever!)

A stash of such gigantic undies,

Each pair could stretch forever!

"We'll take these pants!" the aliens laughed.
But ... *RAAAAR!* They heard loud roars!
And found themselves surrounded by ...

Ginormous dinosaurs!

The dinosaurs were furious.
"Hands off our drawers!"
they roared.
"We'll fight you pesky aliens,
To save our precious hoard!"

The aliens almost fainted!

"DINOSAURS? This can't be so!

You dinos were wiped out from Earth.

Pants-zillion years ago!"

"We hid down here," the dinos said.

"The humans didn't see!

We saved our pants.

but couldn't come out.

We wish we could roam free!"

"We ALL love pants," one alien cheered,
"So there's no need to fight!
I have a plan to get you out
And save you from your plight!"

Those busy aliens got to work,
With laser tools and saws.
They hammered, welded, chopped, and drilled,
Helped by the dinosaurs.

"TA-DA! A super dino-pod
To launch you into space!
We'll take you to our planet.
ZOOM! A most pants-tastic place!"

"Our new home's great!" the dinos said.
"There's underpants for all!"
It's fun the games that can be played
With pants both HUGE and small.

So when your laundry's on the line,
Quick! Guard it on the double.
With aliens AND dinosaurs,
There's twice pants-stealing trouble!